farm next door

hen house

cat

D1506023

Cock~a~Doodle Quack! Quack!

WITHDRAWN

Written by
Ivor Baddiel and Sophie Jubb
Illustrated by Ailie Busby

David Fickling Books

For Hamish,
who always knows what to say
A.B.

For Ruby and Art, who always know
how to wake us up
I.B. & S.J.

A DAVID FICKLING BOOK

Published by David Fickling Books
an imprint of Random House Children's Books
a division of Random House, Inc.
New York

This is a work of fiction. Names, characters, places, and incidents either are the product
of the author's imagination or are used fictitiously. Any resemblance to actual persons, living
or dead, events, or locales is entirely coincidental.

Text copyright © 2007 by Ivor Baddiel and Sophie Jubb
Illustrations copyright © 2007 by Ailie Busby

www.randomhouse.com/kids

Educators and librarians, for a variety of teaching tools, visit us at
www.randomhouse.com/teachers

Library of Congress Cataloging-in-Publication Data
Baddiel, Ivor.
Cock-a-doodle quack! quack! / written by Ivor Baddiel and Sophie Jubb ;
illustrated by Ailie Busby.
p. cm.
SUMMARY: A baby rooster learns through trial and error what sounds he must
crow in the morning to wake up the rest of the farm.
ISBN-10: 0-385-75104-4 (trade) — ISBN-10: 0-385-75105-2 (lib. bdg.)
ISBN-13: 978-0-385-75104-9 (trade) — ISBN-13: 978-0-385-75105-6 (lib. bdg.)
[1. Animal sounds—Fiction. 2. Roosters—Fiction. 3. Animals—Infancy—Fiction. 4. Domestic
animals—Fiction.] I. Jubb, Sophie. II. Busby, Ailie, ill. III. Title.
PZ7.B1373Co 2007
[E]—dc22
2005034590

The illustrations in this book were created using acrylic paints.

MANUFACTURED IN CHINA

10 9 8 7 6 5 4 3 2 1

First American Edition

Once upon a time there was
a baby rooster.

It was his job to wake everybody up in
the morning, but he didn't know how.
He didn't know what to say.

So he went to see the pigs.
"Hello, pigs. It's my job to wake everyone
up in the morning, but I don't know
what to say. What do YOU say?"

"Oink! Oink!" said the pigs.

"That's good," said Baby Rooster.
"I'll try that tomorrow."

The next morning as the sun was rising,
the baby rooster took a deep breath
and at the top of his voice he said,

COCK~A~D

OODLE~OINK~OINK!

But nothing happened.

NOBODY WOKE UP.

So the baby rooster
went to see the cows.

"Hello, cows," he said. "It's my job to wake everyone up in the morning, but I don't know what to say. What do YOU say?"

"Moo! Moo!" said the cows.

"Ooh yes. That's good," said Baby Rooster. "I'll try that tomorrow."

The next morning as the sun was rising,
the baby rooster took a really deep breath and
at the top of his voice he said,

COCK-A-D

OODLE~MOO~MOO!

But nothing happened.

NOBODY WOKE UP.

So he went to see the ducks.
He said, "Hello, ducky ducks. It's my job
to wake everyone up in the morning, but
I don't know what to say. What do YOU say?"

"Quack! Quack!" said the ducks.

"Oh, that's really good," said Baby Rooster.
"I'll try that tomorrow."

The next morning just as the sun was rising,
the baby rooster took a very deep breath
and said,

COCK~A~DOOD

LE~QUACK~QUACK!

But nothing happened.

NOBODY WOKE UP.

The baby rooster was very sad.
"What's the matter?" asked Cat.
Baby Rooster said nothing.

"Oh dear," said the cat. "I can tell something's wrong. You'd better go and see the wise old owl. He'll know what to do."

So Baby Rooster walked up
to the huge barn where Owl lived.
He knocked on the door.
"Come in," said Owl.

"Please can you help me?" said Baby Rooster.
"It's my job to wake everyone up in the
morning, but I don't know what to say."
The wise old owl smiled.
"My friend, tomorrow, as the sun is rising,
go down to the farm gate and sit there quietly.

Don't say anything. Just listen. Then you will know exactly what to do."

That night
Baby Rooster
hardly slept at all.
He was very puzzled.

He still
didn't know
how he was going
to wake everyone up.

At last, the sun began to rise.
The baby rooster got up and
walked down the lane.
He stood on the farm
gate and *listened*
carefully.

It was very quiet. Baby Rooster couldn't hear anything at all. But he remembered the wise old owl's words and he *listened* again.

Then, the baby rooster heard a noise
coming from the farm next door.
He *listened* very, very carefully.
He tried to copy the noise.

COCK-A-

NOODLE~NOO!

NOTHING HAPPENED.

No one woke up.
He *listened* again,
even more carefully.

He took a deep breath.

COCK

~A~POODLE~POO!

STILL NOBODY WOKE UP.

He *listened* as carefully
and as quietly as he could.

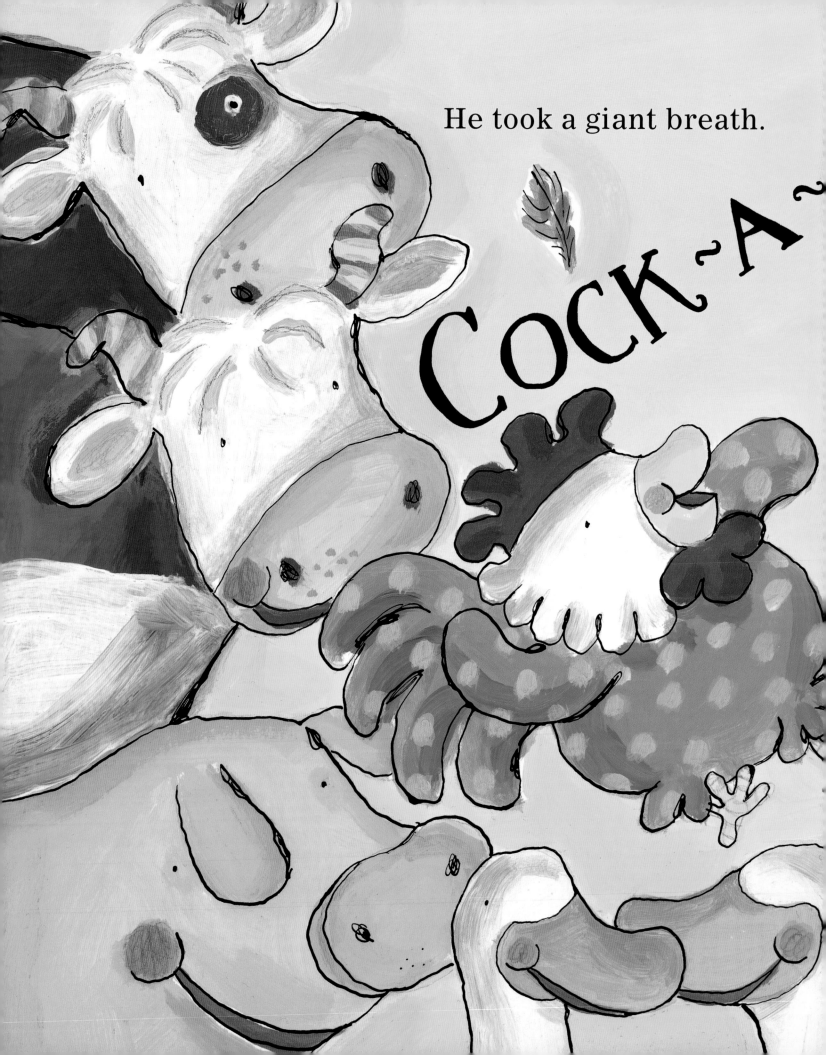

He took a giant breath.

COCK-A-

DOODLE-DOO!

And do you know what happened?

EVERYBODY WOKE UP.

At last Baby Rooster knew how to
wake everybody up.

COCK~A~DOODLE~DOO!

He was so pleased and happy and so tired
that he fell fast asleep.

But he was up early again the next morning. . . .

cows

duck pond

pig sty

farm